The William Shakespeare

CHILDREN'S COLLECTION

Dados Internacionais de Catalogação na Publicação (CIP) de acordo com ISBD

S527r Shakespeare, William
Romeo and Juliet / William Shakespeare. - Jandira, SP : W. Books, 2025..
104 p. ; 12,80cm x 19,80cm. - (Classics).

ISBN: 978-65-5294-206-7

1. Literatura inglesa. 2. Clássicos. 3. Aventura. 4. Fantasia. 5. Imaginação.
I. Título. II. Série.

2025-2507 CDD 823
CDU 821.111

Elaborada por Lucio Feitosa - CRB-8/8803
Índice para catálogo sistemático:
1. Literatura inglesa 823
2. Literatura inglesa 821.111-31

Text based on the original play by William Shakespeare,
adapted by Georgina Brown
Illustrations by Rishabh Goswami

1st edition in 2025
www.cirandacultural.com.br

EASY CLASSICS

William Shakespeare

Romeo & Juliet

W. Books

Romeo Montague

The son of
Old Montague

Old Montague

The head of the
Montague family

Benvolio

Romeo's cousin

Mercutio

A close friend of Romeo

Friar Lawrence

A wise monk

Juliet Capulet

The daughter of Lord and Lady Capulet

Lord and Lady Capulet

The heads of the Capulet family

Tybalt

Juliet's cousin

The Nurse

Juliet's nurse

Count Paris

A wealthy young man

Chapter One

Many years ago, in the beautiful town of Verona, Italy, there lived two families: the Capulets and the Montagues. Both families were very important and incredibly rich. They were also sworn enemies and were always getting into terrible fights with each other.

One sunny day, servants from the Capulet family were walking through the town square when they spotted some of the

Montague servants. They rushed across the street and began fighting, punching and kicking each other in the dusty road.

The Prince of Verona heard the commotion and arrived with his soldiers to break up the fight. 'I am sick and tired

of this feud between the Montagues and the Capulets,' he said angrily. 'It has to stop right now. From this moment on, anyone caught fighting will pay for it with their life.'

The servants hung their heads in shame in front of the prince, while the rest of the town breathed a sigh of relief. The townspeople hoped that, at long last, there would be peace in Verona.

As soon as Old Montague, the head of the Montague family,

feud

A long-standing and nasty quarrel between people or persons.

heard about the fight he hurried into town to search for his son, Romeo. He could only find Benvolio, Romeo's cousin.

'Have you seen Romeo?' Old Montague asked.

'No,' said Benvolio. 'But don't worry, he's far too sensible to get caught up in a fight. I'll go and look for him if you like.'

'Please do,' said Old Montague. 'It would make both his mother and I feel better to know he's safe.'

Soon after, Romeo wandered by and Benvolio told him about what had happened earlier in the streets.

Meanwhile, in another part of town, Lord Capulet was writing invitations for a masked ball at his

house. He made sure to address an invitation to a young man called Paris. Lord Capulet knew Count Paris was in love with his daughter, Juliet, and he planned to introduce them properly at the ball. When he had finished, Lord Capulet gave the invitations to his servant.

‘Make sure you deliver all of them,’ he told the servant. Unfortunately, Lord Capulet did not realise that his servant could not read, and the servant was far too scared to tell him.

Once outside, the servant wandered aimlessly down the street, unsure what to do. Suddenly, he saw Romeo and Benvolio walking towards him and had an idea.

‘Please could you tell me what is written on these pieces of paper?’ he asked.

The servant had no idea that

he was speaking to the son and nephew of Lord Capulet's sworn enemy, Old Montague.

Romeo and Benvolio politely explained what was written on the invites, and the servant thanked them and hurried away.

As soon as he was out of ear shot, Benvolio turned to Romeo. 'Cousin,' he said, 'we should go to that party!'

Romeo thought for a moment. He knew they shouldn't go because of the bad feeling between the two families. If they went, the two cousins could make things even worse. *On the other hand*, he thought, *the party might help me feel better*. Romeo was feeling heartbroken over a young woman called Rosaline, who was not in the least bit interested in him. It was making Romeo miserable.

Benvolio saw that Romeo was unsure. ‘It’s a masked ball,’ he added quickly, ‘so no one will know who we are.’

Romeo agreed, and the two young men went to find their friend Mercutio to invite him to go with them.

Chapter Two

The Capulet's house was filled with excitement as the final preparations were made for the evening's masquerade ball.

Candlelight flickered from every surface, tables groaned under the weight of delicious platters of food and musicians tuned their instruments.

masquerade

A type of party at which the guests wear masks that cover their faces.

Upstairs, Juliet Capulet was getting ready with the help of her nurse.

'You look beautiful,' the nurse told Juliet, stepping back to look at her. 'You will make the loveliest bride one day.'

Suddenly, Lady Capulet swept into the room. 'That is exactly what I wanted to talk to you about,' she said to her daughter, having overheard the conversation. 'What do you think about marriage, Juliet?'

'I haven't really thought about it,' said Juliet, shrugging.

'Well, you need to start thinking about it,' said her mother. 'Many girls your age are married. I'd already given birth to you when I was your age. But to get to the

point, Count Paris would like to marry you.'

The nurse clapped her hands with happiness. 'Juliet!' she gasped. 'He is so handsome.'

'He is coming to the party tonight,' said Lady Capulet.

'If you spend time with him, you will see how wonderful he is and accept his proposal.'

Juliet sighed. 'I'll meet him,' she said. 'But I cannot promise that I'll fall in love.'

There was no time to discuss it any further, the party was about to start. Holding her head high, Juliet left her room and walked down the grand staircase to the ballroom.

Shortly afterwards, Romeo, Benvolio and Mercutio arrived at the party. As Benvolio and Mercutio made their way through the crowd, Romeo spotted the most beautiful girl he had ever seen. He stood still, feet frozen to the floor. Romeo couldn't take his eyes off her, and didn't

even notice when Juliet's cousin, Tybalt, recognised him and rushed to throw him out. Lord Capulet saw his nephew hurrying angrily towards one of the guests

and quickly stepped forward to stop him. 'But, Uncle, there are Montagues here,' hissed Tybalt.

'Let me guess, it's young Romeo,' sighed Lord Capulet.

'Who else?' grumbled Tybalt.

'He's not causing any trouble,' said Lord Capulet. 'Leave him alone. It's a party after all. Try and calm down and have a good time.'

Tybalt was angry but knew better than to argue with his uncle. 'Romeo better watch out the next time I see him,' he muttered under his breath, as Romeo moved through the crowd of party guests.

Meanwhile, Juliet had snuck out of the ballroom to get away from Count Paris. She had met him and wasn't impressed. She could think of nothing worse than marrying him. What Juliet didn't know was that Romeo had been following her, hoping for a chance to speak with her.

Romeo felt nervous as he approached her, shyly reaching out his hand to hers.

'I don't know who you are,' he whispered, 'but I've fallen head over heels in love with you.'

Juliet felt her heart beating fast at the sight of the handsome young stranger in front of her. She knew nothing about this man, except that she had fallen in love with him at first sight.

Romeo leant forward and kissed her gently. 'You kiss perfectly,' Juliet sighed.

Before the pair could speak further, they were interrupted by Juliet's nurse. 'Your mother is looking for you!' she told Juliet. With a final glance over her shoulder at the attractive stranger, Juliet reluctantly made her way back to the ball.

'Who is that?' Romeo asked.

'She's Juliet Capulet,' the nurse replied.

Romeo was devastated. Their families would never allow them to be together. Heartbroken, he left the party and instead of going home, hid in the Capulet's garden.

Romeo hoped that somehow, he might catch one more glimpse of the girl who had captured his heart.

A little while later his patience was rewarded. Juliet stepped out onto her balcony. Romeo thought she was so lovely that even the moon above must be jealous of her beauty. At that moment, Juliet spoke into the night. 'O Romeo, Romeo, wherefore art thou Romeo? Why do you have to be part of the Montague family?'

Romeo stepped forward. He couldn't believe that this beautiful

girl felt the same way as he did. He called up to her. 'I'd do anything for you,' he said. 'I love you.'

Romeo and Juliet talked through the night, finding out everything they could about each other. But the clock was ticking, it would soon be dawn, and Romeo would surely be killed if he was discovered there. 'I'd marry you if I could,' he sighed.

Juliet felt the same. 'But my parents are going to make me marry Count Paris,' she cried. They stared at each other in desperation. Suddenly, Juliet had an idea. 'Our only chance is to get married in secret,' she said.

'Then that's what we'll do,' said Romeo. 'I'll make all the arrangements and send you a message tomorrow.'

Between kisses, Romeo and Juliet quickly said goodnight, knowing they'd see each other the next day.

Chapter Three

After leaving Juliet, Romeo went to see Friar Lawrence, the monk who lived in the countryside. He was a wise man who often helped the people of Verona with medicines and advice.

'Morning, Father,' said a beaming Romeo.

'May God bless you,' replied Friar Lawrence. 'What has put

you in such a good mood, Romeo?'

'I'm in love with Juliet Capulet,' Romeo told him. 'We'd like to get married, but we know our parents will never agree to it.'

Friar Lawrence looked thoughtfully at the young man. He could imagine only too well what Old Montague and Lord Capulet would think of this wedding, but it might help to end their destructive feud. 'Your marriage to Juliet might be just the thing to bring your families together,' he told Romeo. 'Come to my house this afternoon, bring

Juliet and I'll marry you both in secret.'

Romeo could have hugged the old friar; he was so happy.

Meanwhile, Mercutio and Benvolio were busy looking for their friend. Tybalt had sent a letter to Romeo's house challenging him to a duel. The two young men were worried that Tybalt would kill him.

'Romeo is no match for Tybalt,' sighed Mercutio. 'He's absolutely brutal.'

Benvolio shushed Mercutio as a grinning Romeo came into view.

'Where have you been?' asked Benvolio.

'We know you haven't been home all night,' added Mercutio. 'What have you been up to?'

duel

A fight between two people using deadly weapons.

Before Romeo could tell them, Juliet's nurse hurried towards them. 'Do any of you know a young man called Romeo?' she asked. The nurse didn't recognise Romeo without his mask.

'That's me,' said Romeo.

'I need to speak to you privately.'

The pair stepped away from the others. 'Juliet asked me to find you,' the nurse told Romeo. 'But if you intend to hurt her in any way, you'll have me to answer to. She is young and doesn't know much about love.'

‘I promise I’m not going to hurt her,’ said Romeo.

The nurse looked at him and nodded. ‘I think you have a good heart,’ she said.

‘Thank you,’ said Romeo. ‘Tell her to find some way to come to the abbey this afternoon. Friar Lawrence has agreed to marry us.’

‘She’ll be there,’ the nurse said. She rushed away to tell Juliet the good news.

Later that afternoon, Juliet told her parents she was going to see Friar Lawrence to ask for advice about marrying Count Paris. Her parents were delighted and only too happy to let Juliet visit him.

Romeo was already at the abbey talking to the friar.

‘I only hope we don’t regret

this later. Marriage is a sacred thing,' the friar told Romeo. 'No matter what happens, nothing can change the way I feel,' replied Romeo.

'Just be careful,' the friar said. He looked up to see Juliet hurrying into the abbey.

Juliet smiled when she saw the two of them. She was filled with so much love at the sight of Romeo, she thought she might float away with happiness.

sacred

Connected with God or a god; considered to be holy.

‘How are you feeling?’ Romeo asked, taking Juliet's hand.

‘I can’t quite put it into words,’ smiled Juliet, her eyes shining with love. ‘I’m just so happy.’

‘Come on,’ the friar told the couple. ‘Let’s go. I’m not leaving the two of you alone, until you are married.’

And with that, Friar Lawrence joined Romeo and Juliet in marriage.

The newlyweds didn’t have long to celebrate; their love still had to be kept secret. Juliet would have given anything to stay with her new husband but knew she had to return home before her parents got suspicious.

'Don't worry.' Romeo kissed his wife. 'I'll sneak into the gardens tonight and climb onto your balcony so we can spend some time together.'

Counting the hours until they could see each other again, the newlyweds said goodbye. Juliet hurried home, while a beaming Romeo went into town to see his friends. The smile soon slipped from his face when he saw Benvolio and Mercutio arguing with Tybalt in the street.

'What's the problem here?' Romeo asked.

‘You’re my problem,’ growled Tybalt.

‘Come on, it doesn’t need to be like this,’ replied Romeo, who now just wanted to keep the peace with the Capulets. ‘I have nothing against you. Leave me alone.’

‘Well, I have something against you,’ Tybalt said, pulling out his sword. ‘I hope you’re ready to fight!’

‘Right now, I want to make peace,’ sighed Romeo, holding up his hands.

‘Don’t be such a wimp,’ cried Mercutio, who couldn’t understand why Romeo was acting this way. 'If you don't fight him, I will.'

Mercutio drew his sword and lunged towards Tybalt.

'Stop it!' shouted Romeo, trying to break them up. 'Put your swords away!'

‘Cut it out!’ shouted Benvolio, as he and Romeo desperately tried to pull the pair apart. But they were too late. Tybalt slashed his sword at Mercutio, and Romeo gasped in horror as his friend fell to the ground. Romeo rushed to his side and held his friend.

‘This is your fault,’ rasped Mercutio. ‘Your family’s stupid feud with the Capulets has led to this.’

With that, the breath left Mercutio’s body. Romeo stared at his friend in shock. *If it wasn’t for me, this wouldn’t have happened,*

he thought. Heartbroken over his friend's sudden death, Romeo grabbed Mercutio's sword and stabbed Tybalt, who slumped to the ground.

'Romeo, what have you done?' gasped Benvolio. 'People are gathering. The prince will execute you if he finds you. You must get out of here!'

Romeo cried in despair. He had ruined everything! Dropping his sword, he ran for his life.

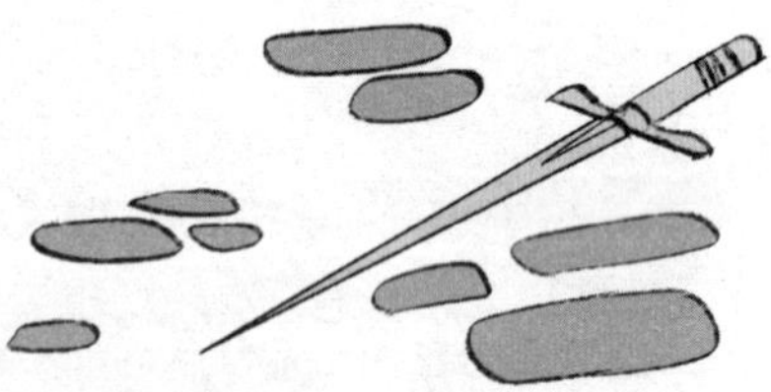

Chapter Four

Shortly afterwards, the Prince of Verona arrived to find Mercutio and Tybalt dead, with Benvolio standing over them. The prince demanded to know what had happened. Benvolio nervously explained, worried that the prince's men would kill Romeo. The prince listened carefully, and thought for a moment before making his decision. 'I can see that Tybalt was mostly to blame for this,' he said.

'Romeo will not die, but he will be banished from Verona.'

Benvolio didn't know how to feel. Being banished was better than being killed, but it meant Romeo would never be able to return to Verona.

The news soon spread throughout the town. As soon as the nurse heard what had happened, she hurried to tell Juliet.

Juliet was heartbroken. 'Cousin Tybalt is dead,' she wailed. 'And

banish

To order somebody to leave a place, especially a country, as a punishment.

I'll never see my husband again.'

'Don't cry,' the nurse begged. 'I've heard that Romeo is hiding at Friar Lawrence's house. Let me go and see him.'

Juliet threw herself into the nurse's arms. 'Please find him for me,' she cried. 'Tell him to come and say goodbye to his wife before he has to leave forever.'

The nurse went to Friar Lawrence's house and knocked on the door. The friar opened it, carefully looking around to make sure no one was watching before he let her in.

'This is a terrible business,' Friar Lawrence said to the nurse, nodding towards Romeo, who was pacing up and down with worry.

'I know,' agreed the nurse. 'I've left Juliet at home sobbing her eyes out.'

'Nurse!' cried Romeo, spotting her. 'How is Juliet?'

'She just cries and cries. She throws herself on her bed and cries for Tybalt and for you. Then she cries some more.'

'This is all my fault! I can't believe I have to leave Verona. My happiness lies with Juliet, wherever she is!'

'Romeo, you should be grateful,' scolded the friar. 'The prince could have had you killed.'

'This is a fate *worse* than death. I might as well be dead if I can't be with Juliet,' Romeo replied.

'Then go and see her tonight, but don't stay long,' said the friar. 'You must go to Mantua and live there until it is safe to come back. Hopefully the prince will forgive you in time, and you will be able to return, happier than before.'

Romeo could only bury his head in his hands. Who knew how long that would take?

That night, Romeo crept through the Capulets' garden and climbed the ivy to Juliet's balcony.

They spent a few happy hours together before Romeo had to leave. He gave his tearful wife one last kiss.

‘I will see you again, won’t I?’ asked Juliet.

‘Of course,’ smiled Romeo. ‘Soon this will be just a horrible memory and we’ll be together again.’

As Romeo climbed down the balcony and ran away through the gardens, Juliet threw herself on her bed and sobbed.

Suddenly her mother and father swept in. ‘Poor Juliet,’ Lady Capulet said, throwing her arms around her daughter. ‘You are still crying over your cousin’s death. Luckily, I have some good news to cheer you up.’

Juliet looked up at her mother. She couldn't imagine anything that would make her feel better right now.

'Your father has decided it's time we had something to celebrate. On Thursday morning, you are going to marry Count Paris.'

Juliet stopped crying and sat up. 'What? No!' she wailed. 'I *can't* marry him.'

'Don't be so silly,' said her father. 'It's all organised.'

'No!' shouted Juliet, jumping to her feet. 'I won't marry him. I don't want to.'

Her father scowled. 'You *will* marry Count Paris on Thursday and I don't want to hear any more of it.'

Shaking their heads in disappointment at Juliet's reaction, her parents left the room.

'What am I going to do?' Juliet asked the nurse. 'I'm already married.'

'You definitely can't tell your parents about Romeo,' said the nurse. 'Perhaps you should just get married again and hope the truth doesn't come out.'

'Okay,' said Juliet, wiping her tears.

'Really?' said the nurse. She hadn't expected Juliet to agree with her so easily.

'Yes, really,' said Juliet, crossing her fingers behind her back. 'Could you let my parents know I'm sorry I made them so angry?'

'Of course,' said the nurse, smiling contently as she left the room.

As soon as the nurse was gone,

Juliet quickly gathered her things, crept down the stairs and ran out the front door. She planned to see Friar Lawrence.

He was the only person in the world who could help her right now.

Chapter Five

Meanwhile, Count Paris was also at Friar Lawrence's, making arrangements for his wedding to Juliet. The friar – who knew that she was already married – was doing his best to delay him, but Paris would not listen.

'You hardly know Juliet,' the friar said. 'Perhaps you should wait, spend some more time with her before committing to such a big thing as marriage.'

'Her father wants to help her feel better after Tybalt's death. I really think marrying me will be a good thing,' Paris replied. Secretly, he couldn't think of a single reason why *any* woman wouldn't want to marry him.

'Speaking of Juliet ...' said the friar, seeing her hurrying towards them.

'It's good to see you, my wife to be,' grinned Paris. 'Are you ready to marry me?'

'As ready as I'll ever be,' Juliet

said. At least it wasn't an actual lie, she supposed.

'Come now, I know you love me,' the count said.

Juliet's eyes widened in desperation, looking at the friar for help.

'Um, I think Juliet would like to speak to me privately,' he told Paris.

'Alright. I know when I'm not wanted. I'll leave you to it,' said the count. 'Until Thursday, Juliet.'

As soon as the door shut behind him, Juliet sank to the floor. 'What am I going to do?' she wailed. 'I'd rather die than marry Paris.'

The friar thought for a moment, his brow furrowed. Suddenly his face cleared.

'I have a suggestion,' he said. 'But it's a pretty drastic one.'

'Believe me, I'd rather do anything than marry Paris. I'll do whatever it takes to stay true to Romeo.'

'Okay.' Friar Lawrence opened his medicine cabinet and picked out a small vial. 'Go home and

vial
A small glass container.

tell your parents that you agree to marry Paris. Then tonight, drink this potion. You will fall into a coma; your body will go cold and it will look like you're dead. But really, you'll be in a deep sleep that will last for two days.'

Juliet stared at him with wide eyes. The friar continued, 'When your parents find you, they will think that you are dead, and you will be put into the Capulets' vault.'

'Then what?' asked Juliet.

vault

A room under a church or in a cemetery, used for burying people.

'I'll send word to Romeo, so he knows about the plan. He and I will be with you when you wake, and the two of you can run away to Mantua and live there together. What do you think?'

'I think it's a brilliant idea,' said Juliet. 'I'll do it.'

'Good luck and stay strong,' said the friar, giving her the potion.

'Thank you.' Juliet clutched the potion in her hand, hoping she was brave enough to go through with the plan.

As soon as she got home, Juliet went straight to her parents. 'I'm sorry I was rude earlier,' she said. 'I was upset about Tybalt. Of course I'll marry Paris.'

'Good girl,' smiled her father.

'He's such a nice man,' added her mother. 'Now go to bed and get some sleep. You're going to need it.'

That night, Juliet sat on her bed and stared at the vial. For a moment, she almost changed her mind. What would happen if Romeo arrived too late or if there wasn't enough air in the vault and she suffocated?

But then she thought about life without Romeo. If drinking the potion meant they could finally be together, it would be worth it. Quickly, before she could change her mind, Juliet uncorked the vial and drank every last bitter drop.

'I love you, Romeo,' she whispered, lying back on her pillow. Within moments, she had fallen into a deep, deep sleep.

Chapter Six

The next morning everything happened just as Friar Lawrence had predicted. The nurse found Juliet's cold body in her bed.

'Juliet's dead!' she screamed.

Lord and Lady Capulet came running. 'Oh, my child!' sobbed Lady Capulet, rushing to hold her daughter in her arms.

'I will never be happy again,' cried Lord Capulet, tears pouring down his cheeks. 'We will no longer have a wedding, but a funeral instead. Change the happy music to sad, the wedding feast to a memorial dinner, and the bridal flowers to a funeral wreath. We will take her body to the family vault.'

Meanwhile, Friar Lawrence had written a letter to Romeo, telling him about the plan. He carefully sealed the envelope and gave it to his trusted friend, Friar John, to deliver it no later than the next day.

However, the news of Juliet's death spread too quickly. People from far and wide heard what had happened. A servant in Mantua hurried to tell Romeo.

'I can't live without her!' Romeo cried. 'I don't *want* to live without her.'

He told the servant to hire him a horse so he could return to Verona.

'But sir, you can't go to Verona,' said the shocked servant. 'You are going to get in trouble. The prince will have you killed if he finds you.'

'Don't worry about me,' Romeo told him. 'Just go and get the things I need.'

While the servant hurried off, Romeo decided what he was going to do. He knew an apothecary who lived in Mantua. 'I will buy a poisoned tonic and go to Juliet's

apothecary

Someone who sells or prepares medicines, now called a pharmacist. Also the name of the place where medicines are sold or prepared, now called a pharmacy.

tomb,' he vowed. 'I'll lie beside her, drink the poison and die. It's the only way we can be together now.'

As soon as the servant returned with a horse, Romeo rode to the apothecary's shop. It was closed, but Romeo banged on the door and shouted until the apothecary opened it.

'I need the deadliest poison you have,' Romeo said.

'I'm not allowed to sell it to you,' said the apothecary. 'It is

tomb

A room, usually underground, where bodies are buried.

against the law in Mantua.'

Romeo was desperate. He could see the apothecary was poor and offered him more money than he could ever earn. The man quickly handed over the bottle of poison before he could change his mind.

'If you put this in any liquid and drink it, you will certainly die,' the apothecary warned him. 'It is strong enough to kill twenty men.'

Romeo thanked him and carefully put the bottle of poison in his bag. He jumped onto his horse and rode towards Verona as fast as he could.

Friar John had returned to Friar Lawrence's house.

'How is Romeo?' Friar Lawrence asked his friend. 'Do you have a letter from him for me?'

'I didn't get to see him,' said Friar John. 'Before I left, I visited the sick, but I was put into isolation in case the illness spread. I wasn't able to go.'

'So, who took the letter?'

'No one. I still have it. I couldn't

even send a messenger! I'm sorry.'

Friar Lawrence stared at his friend in horror. 'I can't even imagine what Romeo will do if he has heard that Juliet is dead. There's no time to explain, get me a crowbar as fast as you can.'

As Friar John hurried off, Friar Lawrence shook his head in despair. He felt sick. He had a horrible sense that something awful was going to happen – he could feel it in his bones.

'I must go to the vault,' Friar Lawrence muttered to himself. 'Juliet will be awake in three hours. I'll write to Romeo again, then hide Juliet here until he arrives.'

Count Paris had also decided to pay his respects at Juliet's tomb that night. He left his horse with his servant and carried some flowers to lay at the tomb. As he was leaving, he saw Romeo breaking into the vault.

'Stop!' he shouted. 'How dare you! You killed Juliet's cousin and caused her to die of grief.'

'Leave me alone,' growled Romeo. 'I loved her more than you ever could.'

'Then you give me no choice but to arrest you!' cried Paris, pulling out his sword.

'I'm here to kill *myself*, not you,' Romeo replied. 'I warn you; I have nothing to lose in fighting you.'

'This is not going to end well,' sighed the count's servant, who

was watching from the shadows. 'I had better go and get the police.' He jumped on the count's horse and galloped away just as Paris

lunged at Romeo, who angrily fought back.

Moments later, Romeo struck Paris with his sword. Paris cried

out, falling to his knees. 'I am dying,' he gasped, clutching his stomach. 'Please, Romeo, grant my final wish and lay me next to Juliet.'

Romeo lifted the count and carried him into the tomb. Placing him carefully on the ground near Juliet's body, as Paris took his last breath.

Romeo looked longingly at the love of his life, his eyes filled with sadness. As he knelt beside her, Romeo picked up Juliet's motionless hand and kissed her cheek, which was as cold as the tomb that surrounded her.

'I will never leave you again,' he whispered, before opening the bottle of poison and drinking it

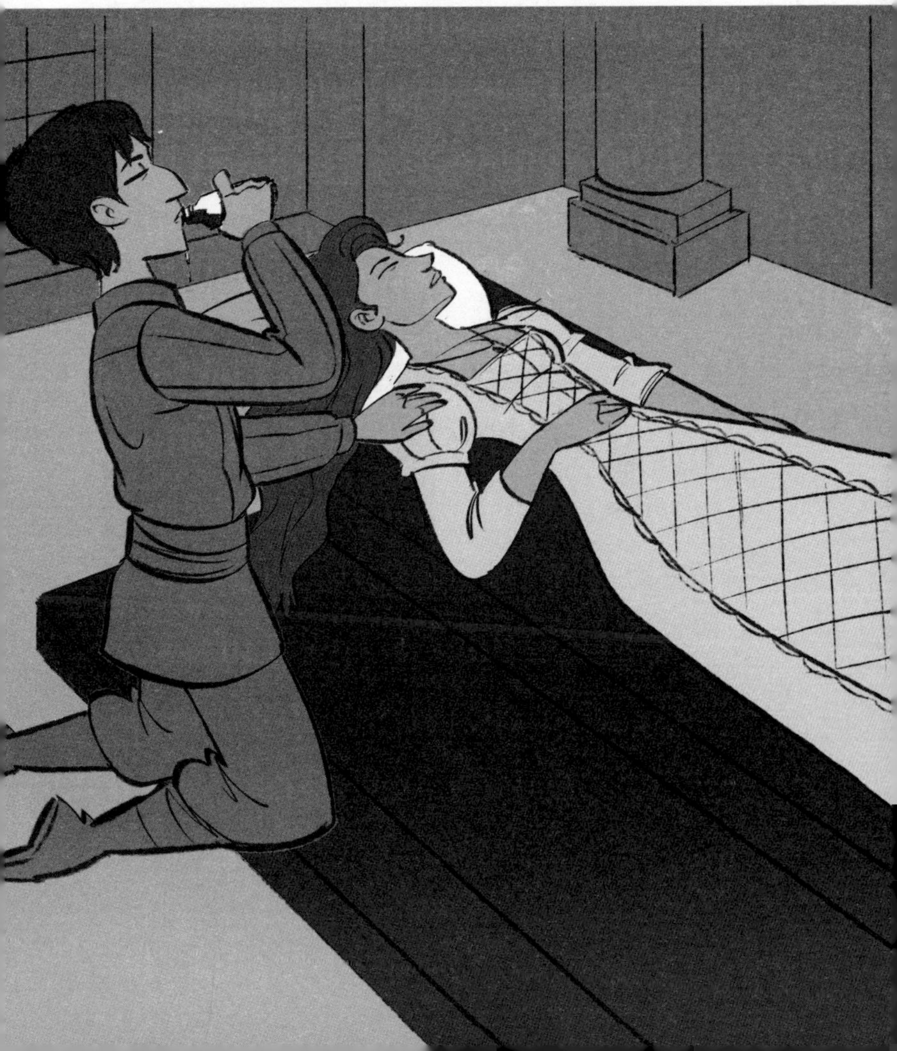

all. He leant over and kissed Juliet one last time. 'Goodbye, my love,' he said. In just a few moments, Romeo lay still.

Just as Romeo took his final breath, Friar Lawrence ran into the tomb. He had seen the swords and blood stains outside and

knew something dreadful had happened.

'Romeo!' he cried, hurrying to the young man's side. 'And Paris too!' he cried, seeing the count's body. He sank to the floor, horrified that his plan had gone so terribly wrong.

Juliet began to stir. She rubbed her eyes and sat up. *Where am I?* she wondered. Then she saw the friar and remembered his plan.

'Where is Romeo?' she whispered, then cried out when she saw his lifeless body next to her. Sobbing, she threw her arms around him.

'Juliet!' cried the friar, trying to pull her away from Romeo. 'There's no time, we have to get out of here! A servant has already gone for the police. They mustn't find us here!'

'I'm not leaving,' said Juliet, 'I won't leave Romeo.'

With a last desperate look at the terrible scene, the friar hurried from the tomb.

Juliet kissed Romeo's lifeless face over and over again, until she saw the bottle of poison in his hand and realised what he had done. 'I have nothing left to live for,' she whispered, stroking his cheek. She picked up the bottle of poison and shook it. It was empty. In desperation, Juliet kissed

Romeo's cold lips, hoping that some of the poison would rub onto her own.

Suddenly she heard a noise.

Someone was coming.

Juliet grabbed Romeo's dagger. 'I don't want to live without you, Romeo,' she cried, before plunging it into her heart and collapsing on top of him.

The police cautiously entered the tomb, followed by Count Paris's servant and a trembling Friar Lawrence. But they were too late ...

Romeo and Juliet were dead.

When the Prince of Verona heard what had happened, he

summoned Friar Lawrence, the Capulets and the Montagues.

A sorrowful Friar Lawrence told them the terrible story from the beginning. 'I am happy to be punished for my part in it,' he said, wringing his hands in sorrow.

The prince shook his head in sadness.

'This is what happens when families hate each other,' said the prince. 'Romeo and Juliet have paid the price for your feud.'

Wiping away his tears, Lord Capulet stepped forward and offered his hand to a sobbing

Old Montague. 'Let's never fight again,' he said. They agreed to build a statue of Romeo and Juliet in the town centre, in honour of their love and as a reminder of the tragedy that had come upon their families.

‘This is a terrible way to finally have peace,’ said the prince. ‘For never was a story of more woe, than this of Juliet and her Romeo.’